The Indigo-Eyed Pup

a short story

Judy Lunsford

The Indigo-Eyed Pup

a short story

Judy Lunsford

Nicolas woke to the sound of hunters calling out to one another in the darkness. At first, he tried to sleep through it, rolling over and trying to kick the too short blanket over his feet. But it was no use, if he pulled the blanket up high, it left his feet uncovered. If he pulled it lower on the bed with his toes, to cover his feet, his shoulders lay exposed to the cold.

It wasn't the first time the hunters had been on his land, and he usually didn't mind. They kept the predators' numbers down and kept the deer from eating all of his herb garden.

He tried to go back to sleep, but the yelping of the great wolves roused him from the semi-warmth of his bed.

This would not do.

Nicolas swung his feet over the side of the bed and waved his hand in the pitch black that filled his hut.

Several candles lit around the room, giving him enough light to see by.

He slid his feet into his slippers and felt his joints ache in the cold biting air. He reached to the end of his bed and pulled on his fur-lined robe. It didn't make his old aching joints feel any better, but it kept the bite of the night air off of his skin.

He stood up and shuffled across the room, letting the wooden floorboards help him get his slippers all the way settled on his feet.

He picked up a lantern and it lit as he touched it.

The papers from his latest project lay strewn all over the table. As he picked up the lantern, a few pages fluttered to the floor. He made a mental note to organize his table so he could find the things he needed when the time came to conduct his experiments.

But there was a more pressing need at the moment. The need for the final piece to his upcoming work. The final piece that would lead to his own end, and a new beginning.

He went to the door and opened it.

A rush of cold air hit him as the outside air tried to make its way inside the hut. The smell of the conifer trees helped to wake him up, as the fresh smell of trees always did. He found forest living to be quite invigorating.

He pulled his robe tighter around himself and waved his hand at the fireplace from the doorway.

He must have been asleep for a long while to let the fire go down. But that was usually the result of one of his visions. He could have been asleep for days at this point. He was just happy he hadn't frozen to death in the meantime.

But he knew that no matter how long he slept, he wouldn't have died. Because this was the night the visions spoke of, he was sure of it. The visions were never wrong.

He stepped out into the darkness and listened carefully.

The hunters were not too far to the west of him, and they were in pursuit.

The yelps and growls of the wolves told him that the hunters had gotten one. Most likely the mother. She was the first to die in his visions.

He could hear the pups as the hunters got them as well.

Nicolas knew he had to move quickly.

He ran off his tiny porch in front of his little hut and out into the darkness. Towards the sounds of the hunters.

The ground was hard and cold beneath his slippers and he lost his footing more times than he would have liked.

He grumbled to himself, wishing he had taken the time to put on his boots. But in his sleep-filled hurry, he hadn't thought about it until it was now too late to go back for them.

Nicolas could hear the pup already. He had to find him.

This pup would be the last of his kind, and the gods had great things in store for him.

He made his way to the edge of the woods that surrounded his tiny wooden hut.

The coniferous trees were calling to him. Instructing him where to go to find the pup. They led him further into the darkness and closer to the hunters.

He could hear the hunters battling the adult wolves of the pack.

And he knew that the wolves would lose.

The humans had been at odds with the wrong wolves.

The gray wolves were the ones sneaking into the villages at night, stealing small children from their beds. But the humans had no cares about whether or not they were hunting down the wrong wolves. They wanted to hunt them all, the great black wolves included.

Nicolas held up his lantern. He could hear two pups coming his way.

The small black creatures ran straight towards him and his lantern light.

Nicolas held the lantern high and looked for the sign that his vision had shown him.

The first pup came towards him and looked up at him with dark brown frightened eyes.

A smaller pup came up behind him.

He held the lantern down towards them both.

The smaller one looked up at him as if he had known Nicolas for ages. The iridescent indigo eyes stared up at him and he nearly jumped into the old man's arms.

Nicolas picked up the indigo eyed pup.

He could hear the hunters coming their way.

"Another one went this way," he could hear them calling to one another.

He looked at the brown eyed pup.

"May your sacrifice someday be worth it," Nicolas said to the pup on the ground. "I'm so sorry."

He turned and headed back to his hut with the indigo-eyed pup.

The other pup tried to follow, but he was too tired and couldn't keep up with the wizard's long strides.

He left the pup behind, without looking back, and extinguishing his lantern, he disappeared into the darkness.

The hunters found the pup moments later and the pack was brought to an end. Or so the hunters thought.

Nicolas went into his hut with tears in his eyes and looked down at the indigo-eyed pup that he held in his arms. He listened to the hunters congratulating themselves on ending the threat of the wolves. As they headed back towards the town, they began to sing a victory cheer, not knowing that one single pup had managed to escape.

"You are now the last of your kind," Nicolas said.

The pup wiggled closer to Nicolas's chest for warmth.

"Your destiny is now set in motion."

*

It had been several months since the hunters had ended the great black wolves and hunted them to extinction.

With the exception of the indigo-eyed pup that Nicolas had been secretly raising.

The gray wolves had moved on, as they always did, and the humans foolishly congratulated themselves on ending the wolf threat on their village.

But Nicolas knew better.

He knew the gray wolves would someday return.

But that wasn't his concern.

His concern was that now, the destiny of many relied on the survival of the indigo-eyed pup.

Nicolas had been leaving the pup alone in his hut for a short time now and then. Gradually lengthening his departures for longer and longer periods of time. When he was sure the pup could be left alone without howling for a matter of hours, Nicolas made his first venture into town in months. Or possibly years.

There were supplies he needed.

He entered the small town and was alarmed at how crowded it was growing.

The edges of the town reached further into the forest than he remembered and as he made his way through the hustle and bustle of the busy streets, it was a while before he saw anything familiar. It wasn't until he reached the merchant streets that things started looking the way he recognized what was once a very small town.

He entered the herbalist's shop and a small bell filled the air with a metallic jingle and announced his presence. His nose was greeted by the familiar scents of many herbs and spices, most of which he was very familiar with. It smelled like the comfort of home to him.

The shopkeeper, MacMillian, came out from the back and smiled when he saw Nicolas.

"Long time no see, old man," MacMillian said cheerfully.

"You're one to talk," Nicolas said.

MacMillian was starting to show his age. His hair was longer and grayer than the last time Nicolas had been here. And the wrinkles on his face were deeper and more pronounced than Nicolas remembered them being.

"How long has it been?" Nicolas asked.

He no longer trusted his own sense of time. He had been alone in the forest for too long.

"I haven't seen you in at least two years," MacMillian said. "Maybe even three now."

"Has it been that long?" Nicolas muttered. "Seems like it's only been as many months."

"Time blends together when you live out in the wilds," MacMillian said.

"So, it does," Nicolas said.

He walked up to the counter and placed a neatly written list before MacMillian.

"This is what I need," Nicolas said.

"That's quite a list," MacMillian said as he read down through the items.

"Like you said," Nicolas said. "It's been almost three years."

"I can get you all of these," MacMillian said. "But it will take me some time."

"I will stop in at the grocer's and come back then," Nicolas said.

"I'll have it ready by the time you return," MacMillian said as he started scurrying around to gather the items.

Nicolas waved and headed out the door. The jingle of the bell filled the air once again and Nicolas made his way out onto the busy street.

The smell of mud and horses assailed his nose.

He made his way down the bustling street and went into the grocer's market. He didn't recognize anyone who worked there, so he busied himself gathering his own items.

Flour, sugar, and other things he needed piled into his basket. He took it all up to the counter and the merchant added up his purchases.

Nicolas quietly paid and left quickly.

No one but the merchant seemed aware of his presence. And Nicolas had intended it to be that way.

Within minutes, the only record or memory the merchant would have of Nicolas' visit would be the receipt for the purchases that lay in the stack on the counter.

Nicolas went back to the herbalist's shop and MacMillian was just finishing up his order when he came through the jingling door.

"I'm just finishing up the last of it," MacMillian said.

He tucked a few brown paper wrapped items on top of the pile.

Nicolas looked at his groceries and the wrapped packages on the counter and wondered how he would manage to carry all of it home.

"I'll get you another basket," MacMillian said.

The gray headed man slipped into the back and reemerged with a basket that he started filling with all of Nicolas's order.

"Thank you kindly," Nicolas said. "I didn't realize how much I would be buying today."

Nicolas opened the bag on his hip and looked at the remaining coins inside.

"How much do I owe you?" Nicolas asked.

"Your money's no good here, old man," MacMillian said.

Nicolas looked up at the man and blinked blankly. "What do you mean?"

MacMillian leaned over the counter and gestured for Nicolas to come closer.

Nicolas stepped up to the counter and leaned his ear towards the shopkeeper.

"You're not the only one with visions," MacMillian said.

Nicolas stepped back and looked at MacMillian. He could feel a cold shiver run through his body.

"What do you know?" Nicolas asked.

"I know nothing," MacMillian smiled at Nicolas and shrugged. "I did, however, add a large bone with lots of marrow to your order. Just in case the need for its use arises."

Nicolas stared at MacMillian, still not knowing what to make of the situation. The possession of a black wolf could mean imprisonment or death. He did not like the fact that someone else might know of the indigo-eyed pup's existence.

"Don't worry, your secret is safe with me," MacMillian said. "Don't think that you are alone in this. I have my part to play as well. Just know that if danger comes, you have a friend."

"Thank you," Nicolas said. He stared at MacMillian for a moment longer before nodding and saying again, "Thank you."

Nicolas took the basket off the counter and headed out of the shop, one basket over the crook of each arm.

He set out onto the bustling street once again, wishing that the town hadn't grown so much since his last visit.

He made his way to the edge of town and sat to rest for a moment before heading back to his hut in the center of the forest.

He thought about the words of his friend, McMillian.

Nicolas wondered who else might have visions beside him. And if they would all be allies, or if some would some be a threat to him and the pup.

He gathered his belongings and headed back on his way into the forest.

Nicolas was so lost in thought, he didn't realize that there was a flock of silent crows following him home.

*

When Nicolas arrived back at his hut, the pup leapt to his feet when the old man came in through the door.

The puppy was getting rather large and was wagging his long black tail with happiness that the man was home. Nicolas was thrilled to see that everything in his hut was intact, and that the wolf had been well behaved while he was out.

Nicolas set his baskets on the table and then pet the wolf happily. He gave the wolf a solid pat on the back and then turned to the herbalist's basket.

"I think there might be a present here for you, Indigo," Nicolas said.

He rummaged around until he found the bone shaped package.

Indigo's eyes widened when he smelled the package and snatched the brown paper wrapped parcel out of Nicolas's hands before he could get the paper off.

Nicolas watched with amusement as Indigo took it to his favorite spot in front of the fireplace and tore the paper off with glee.

Nicolas laughed as the dog made a mess of the paper and then laid down on it as if it didn't exist to start in on his bone.

"Why don't you take that outside?" Nicolas suggested, opening the door for the wolf.

Indigo picked up the bone and ran through the door and, after doing a short amount of business, laid down on the porch happily, gnawing away at the bone.

Nicolas propped the door open so he could keep an eye on the pup and started to pick up the pieces of brown paper that the dog had strewn around on the floor. He was about to throw the paper into the fire when he noticed that there was writing on some of it.

He hadn't noticed the writing before, because the writing had been on the inside of the wrapping paper.

Nicolas found all of the pieces with writing and sat down at the table to piece the message together.

The message was short, but direct. And Nicolas was certain that it came from MacMillian, the herbalist, to him.

It said:

Beware the crows. They report back to one who should not know.

Nicolas got up quickly and went outside.

He stood next to the pup while he happily gnawed on the bone, holding it steady with his front paws as if they were hands.

Nicolas looked around and saw several crows sitting on his fence that he had built to protect his herb garden. A few more sat in the conifer trees in the distance.

Nicolas raised his hands and chanted a few words in the old dialect.

The crows burst into flames and fizzled to the ground in a mist of black ash.

"Inside," he commanded the wolf. "Let's take that inside by the fire."

The pup obediently took the bone into the hut and laid down happily by the fire and continued gnawing on the bone.

The wizard glanced at the pieces of the note again and shook his head.

He gathered up the pieces of paper with the message on it and tossed them into the fire. His friend went to lengths to hide the message, so he wasn't about to leave evidence of it laying around.

Nicolas watched the pup as he continued gnawing on the bone, completely oblivious to everything else around him.

Nicolas went over to the table and started unloading his purchases. He lovingly took each item out of the baskets and laid them on the table.

He started to unwrap each item and took care as he put away the items that needed no preparation for storage. Once the flour, sugar, and other items were neatly in their places, he looked at the array of items that needed to be stored in a more magical manner.

He spent the afternoon preparing tinctures and storing the magical items in a proper manner for each one.

When he was done with that, there remained only a few items left on the table. He glanced up at the pup, who was now laying belly up by his bone, sound asleep and panting happily.

Nicolas started preparing the remaining ingredients for making tea.

This wasn't any ordinary tea, and Nicolas treated it as such. He carefully measured out the exact amounts of the different herbs and spices for the tea. He meticulously wrapped them in a cloth bundle and then took the kettle off the fire.

He poured the hot water into a clean bowl and then set the kettle aside. He put the little bundle of herbs into the tea and as it steeped, he chanted the words of a spell that he had been spending the last few months putting together and memorizing.

The smell of the tea was worse than he thought it would be. He hoped that wouldn't be a problem. He swirled the bag of herbs around clockwise before taking it out of the tea, wringing out as much water as he could, and then tossing the drained bag into the fire.

The bag went up into a puff of indigo smoke and the smoke drifted out of the fire and slowly wafted over to the wolf who was still asleep on the floor.

The smoke encircled the wolf and as it came up to the wolf's nose, the smoke slowly drifted up into the animal's nostrils as he breathed in the indigo smoke.

The wolf woke up and looked over at Nicolas with his indigo eyes.

"You need to drink this as well," Nicolas said to the wolf.

He picked up the bowl of tea and brought it over to the wolf and set it on the floor in front of him.

Indigo sat up and sniffed the bowl. He made a face, licking his nose and looking at Nicolas.

"I know it smells bad," Nicolas said. "But you need to drink it down. "

The wolf sniffed it again and looked at Nicolas.

"Go on," Nicolas said. "Drink up."

The wolf sighed and then set to lapping up the tea from the bowl.

He stopped several times to gag and lick his mouth distastefully. But after a few minutes, the wolf had emptied the bowl of the tea.

Nicolas picked up the bowl and set it on the table and then went back over to sit with the wolf in front of the fire.

The wolf gagged a few more times. Nicolas was afraid the wolf would throw up the tea, thus nullifying its effects, but the wolf managed to keep the tea down.

"It's all right," Nicolas stroked the wolf down the length of his long silky back. "The taste will go away soon, but the effects should be permanent."

The wolf gagged again and then looked up at Nicolas.

"That tasted terrible," the wolf said.

Nicolas stared at the wolf for a moment, in shock, and then began to laugh.

"It worked," he said gleefully.

"Of course it worked," Indigo said. "You've been laboring over that spell forever."

"You can talk," he grabbed Indigo by the head and scratched him behind the ears.

"I can talk?" Indigo repeated. He pulled his head away from Nicolas. "You can understand me?"

"Yes," Nicolas laughed and clapped his hands together. "Yes, I can understand you."

"Well, this just made things a lot easier," Indigo said.

"That, my dear pup," Nicolas smiled. "Was the point."

*

Time passed and Nicolas spent his days teaching Indigo everything that the pup would need to know.

When he felt the pup was ready, he told him what really happened the night that Nicolas found Indigo and rescued him from the hunters.

It took Indigo some adjustment when he learned that he was the last of his kind, but Nicolas gave him the space he needed and time to grieve.

One evening, by the fire, as they shared a meal, Nicolas felt it was time to tell Indigo of his visions.

"There will come a time, in the near future, where you will be on your own," Nicolas said. "You will need to take what you have learned from me and seek out your own visions and follow them."

"I don't want to go without you," Indigo said. "Why can't you come with me/"

"I would if I could," Nicolas said. "But the visions have told me that you will be on your own. I must sacrifice myself to save you."

"No," Indigo shook his head. "I don't like this vision. I don't want any if that's what they say."

"You have no voice in the matter," Nicolas said. "The visions will always come true."

"Then I refuse to have any," Indigo said.

Nicolas laughed softly to himself, "If only it were that easy."

Indigo pricked up his ears and listened to the sounds of the forest outside.

"I hear more crows," he said.

"Beware the crows," Nicolas said. "They will betray you to those who wish you dead."

Indigo sighed. "There are so many of them."

"I know," Nicolas said. "Remember the chant I taught you. It will burn the ones who have been sent to harm you. The rest are just simple birds."

"I'll remember," Indigo said.

Nicolas reached down and scratched Indigo under the chin. The wolf lifted his nose high into the air and let the old man scratch him for as long as he would.

Nicolas stopped and pat Indigo on the head and looked down at the dog.

"I think it's time we got some sleep," he said.

He and the dog climbed onto the bed. Nicolas pulled the blanket close up around his shoulders and Indigo laid down on Nicolas's cold feet.

Nicolas sighed with happiness, even though he knew that tonight was the night that his visions had shown him. He loved the nights with warm feet and a happy dog on them.

*

Indigo dreamed of a red dragon. He travelled alone and was on a quest. The quest was what Indigo was destined to resolve. He must find the dragon and help the dragon find the sword. The Blood Moon Sword that had been stolen from the red dragons.

He and the young red dragon were destined to save the world.

Indigo woke up and looked over at the old man.

He knew that he had just had his first vision. And it did not include the man who had cared for him all this time.

Indigo raised his nose into the air. The faint scent of smoke and burning trees came drifting in through the windows from outside.

Indigo rose up and went to the window. He looked out and saw the trees glowing with orange fire.

"Get up," Indigo bounced on the old man. "Get up now."

Nicolas sat up and looked at the wolf.

"The time has come," he said. "You must run. Go now."

"Not without you," Indigo said. "I won't leave you behind."

"You must," Nicolas said. "This night has been foreseen, and my time is at an end."

"Only if you let it," Indigo said. "Get up, now."

Nicolas jumped out of bed and pulled on his boots and a warm coat.

He led the wolf to the door and opened it for him.

"Go, now," Nicolas said. "I will be right behind you."

"Promise?" Indigo said.

Nicolas looked down at the wolf and smiled, "I promise. I just need to get a weapon."

He held the door for the wolf.

"Go now," Nicolas said. "Scout a clear path for our escape."

Indigo bolted out the door and through the front yard, accidentally stepping on the old man's herb garden as he went.

He tried to sidestep around it, but he was in too much of a rush to get away from the fire that was quickly encroaching onto the backside of the hut.

Indigo turned and waited for the old man to come outside.

When he did, Indigo shouted over the roar of the flames.

"This way," Indigo called out. "Come this way."

The old man had his staff and was heading around to the wrong side of the house.

"Wait," Indigo called out. "Come back."

He took a few steps back towards the hut, but then a giant creature came through the fire from the woods. It was a flaming demon that had its eyes fixed on Nicolas.

Indigo ran towards the old man, as Nicolas raised his staff and cast a spell to damage the demon creature.

Indigo could feel the heat of the flames as they licked from the treetops and burning embers rained down on the roof of their little hut.

Nicolas and the demon, engaged in battle, didn't notice Indigo's approach.

He ran towards the battle, and over to the old man's side.

"Run," Nicolas said to the dog. "Don't look into the creature's eyes, or he will be able to track you wherever you go. Run, now!"

"How can I help?" Indigo asked.

"You can help by running to safety!" Nicolas screamed at the dog.

He lifted his hand towards the wolf and gave him a soft zap of lightning that filled the air with a sharp crack and stung Indigo on the shoulder.

He yelped in pain and turned to run.

He ran as fast as his legs would carry him and into the woods on the other side of the forest, angling away from the town that he knew was to the northeast.

Indigo ran until he collapsed from exertion and he lay in the forest, fast asleep until the sunlight coming through the trees in dappled patches woke him up.

He retraced his steps through the forest and made his way back to the only place he had ever called home.

The tiny hut had burned completely to the ground and the herb garden had burned as well.

Indigo went out towards the trees where the demon creature had been battling the old man.

Laying in the charred remains of the edge of the forest, was Nicolas. His body was lifeless and severely burned. Indigo approached him and hoped that he wasn't dead.

Indigo sniffed him, searching for any hope of life, and nudged the man's shoulder with a front paw.

"Please, wake up," Indigo said. "I can't do this without you."

The spirit of the old man appeared in the woods and walked towards the wolf. His blue luminescence glowing, even in the daylight.

"Indigo," he said. "You must go now."

"Come with me," Indigo begged.

"I cannot," Nicolas said. "For I have other places I need to be."

"I can't do this without your help," Indigo said. "I don't know what to do."

"Follow your visions," Nicolas said. "Find the red dragon. I will be with you when you need me most. But until then, I must continue to battle the demon creature until you are far away from here."

"He's not dead?" Indigo asked.

"Far from it," Nicolas said. "It will come for you and it can only be killed with the Blood Moon Sword."

"That's what the dragon is looking for?" Indigo asked.

Nicolas nodded.

"Go, follow your destiny, find the sword, and then avenge me," Nicolas said.

"How?" Indigo said. "I have no way to use a sword."

"You will find a way," Nicolas said. "Now go. Find your dragon. Leave here and don't look back."

Indigo watched as Nicolas faded away into the trees.

The wolf turned back towards the unburned forest and ran.

More books by Judy Lunsford:

Gamers
Schemers

Fire Lily
Bezbell
Kirog
Fire Lily Omnibus

Moonlight Magic
Moonlight Melody

The Red Dart
Shadow Mountain

The Portal Wars
The Grimoires

For YA:
Life Unscripted
The Secret Gondal Society

Thank you for reading.
If you enjoyed this book, you can find more stories
at
JudyLunsford.com
or your favorite online retailer.